DO NOT REMOVE
CARDS FROM POCKET

Life Riddles

MELROSE COOPER

Life
Riddles

HENRY HOLT

New York

Henry Holt and Company, Inc.
Publishers since 1866
115 West 18th Street
New York, New York 10011

Henry Holt is a registered
trademark of Henry Holt and Company, Inc.

Published in Canada by Fitzhenry & Whiteside Ltd.,
195 Allstate Parkway, Markham, Ontario L3R 4T8.
Library of Congress Cataloging-in-Publication Data
Cooper, Melrose.
Life riddles / by Melrose Cooper.
p.   cm.
Summary: Twelve-year-old Janelle, a talented writer, uses her
skills to help her cope with her family's problems.
[1. Authorship—Fiction. 2. Family life—Fiction. 3. Family problems—
Fiction. 4. Afro-Americans—Fiction.] I. Title.
PZ7.C78746Li 1993   [Fic]—dc20   93-30708

ISBN 0-8050-2613-4

First Edition—1993

Printed in the United States of America on acid-free paper. ∞

1   3   5   7   9   10   8   6   4   2

In memory of R. Donald Brocious
(1941–1993):
gift-giver, riddle-resolver, hero to hundreds,
with longing and love
—M. C.

Life Riddles

ONE

A swarm of butterflies was flapping away in my stomach. The couldn't-wait feeling had ahold of me good. The radio didn't help, the television either, with Mama and my baby sisters due home from work and Latchkey any minute and me wanting to tell them all about beating Leonard Williams in the essay contest for the third year in a row. Aching to tell them how I was probably going to get the shiny gold trophy on Awards Day in June, not Leonard Williams, even though it was only October now, because nobody had ever won three years in a row and I had more poetry points than anyone else in the whole seventh grade, too. Dying, actually, to scream "I'm the winner!" soon as Mama opened the door.

Boy, would they all be proud when they found

out I wrote the best piece, called "Where I'd Go to Follow My Dreams," I thought. Mama would burst, I knew. Crystal would see then how keeping a journal every day pays off. Maybe, I hoped, she'd even stop saying "Do you *have* to write *everything* down?" every night. Maybe Roxann'd stop complaining about the light being left on for an extra fifteen minutes.

I ran to my room to find my essay copy. I opened my top dresser drawer where I kept all my important things. It was right under the card I got from Daddy for my birthday last month. Seeing that kicked my daydreams into high gear.

I wondered where he was and what he was doing right that very minute. I wondered if he ever thought about me at the same split second I was thinking about him, like right now.

How many minutes went by I don't know when finally I heard footsteps coming up the apartment stairs. Closer. Closer. I flung the door wide and yelled "Mama!" then swallowed back her name fast as I had sung it out.

It was nobody's mama and nobody's baby sisters standing there. It was the meter man from the electric company with a shut-off notice for Mama.

He explained that this was it. The first notice, he said, had gone unheeded. Unheeded. Well, I know Mama, and she wouldn't unheed a message like that. She might not be able to pay right on time, but that's not the same thing.

Last time it was the phone. She was putting a little bit away each week for it to get back on.

That electric man went downstairs. Next thing I knew, the radio and TV died, right along with my excitement.

I sunk down into the green beanbag and thought about how it was before Daddy lost his job and we lost Daddy soon after. With him and Mama quarreling all the time, I used to be wishing on stars and rabbits' feet and lucky clovers that he'd just leave. Since he'd been gone, I'd been rewishing all the time with just my plain heart and soul for him to come back.

That's how life is, Aunt Barbara says. I should have listened to her saying, "Be careful what you wish for; it might come true."

Aunt Barbara was full of life riddles. Some she made up, and some she got elsewhere. I never understood them till something happened to point things out.

When Daddy was here, times were tough. We scrimped and scrounged. We never had a car. Still don't. We wore our jeans till the knees poked through, then turned them into shorts. Same with our sneakers and the toes. We didn't have a lot, just like now, but at least we had a daddy.

I heard the footsteps, the right ones this time. Right footsteps, wrong message. Before Mama even took off her coat, I blurted out, "The man from the electric been here."

My baby sisters knew the meaning of that.

"Mama, can I sleep with you tonight?" whined Roxann. She was five and scared of the dark.

"Sure, baby," Mama said.

"Yippee, I can't do my homework!" Crystal cheered. Crystal was nine, three years younger than me, but she wasn't near as mature acting. Aunt Barbara had a life riddle for that, too. She said, "The older you are, the older you are." I guess that had something to do with me being firstborn.

Mama slumped into the flower-print chair. Her face got dark underneath her blush. I felt guilty giving her the news, almost like I was the one that shut off the power.

I wanted to say "I take it back," but even if I took back the words, it would make no difference to the radio or television.

Mama allowed herself one minute of slumping. Then she straightened up and said, "Come on, pioneer ladies. Round up them tallow candles and some matches while I stoke the hearth for our fire."

Super-Duper Stupid, I mumbled under my breath. Pioneer ladies, sure. Well, we weren't living in covered wagons in the olden days, and I hated pretending about it. You could call it any name and play a cute game about it, but it still came out Modern-Day Suffering in my mind.

I was at an age where worry starts to stick, and events like this one worried me bad. The feeling kept me squirming uncomfortably, like there was an army of inchworms crawling all over my skin.

"Candles, Crystal," I said. "You know what that means."

She figured it out. "Hush, Janelle," she said. "I forgot about that. Ain't no TV without the electric anyway, so I can't watch programs instead of homework. Shoot."

And I can write in my journal. Ha ha, I thought.

Crystal turned to Roxann. "Let's get them candles," she said. Those two ran off in the spirit again.

They look like twins, my sisters, except for their sizes. Teachers we had and tenants who know us for just a little while are always calling Crystal Roxann and Roxann Crystal. Roxann and Crystal say "hello" politely anyway like Mama tells them.

They look like Daddy and Mama both, funny as that sounds. They both have wide brown eyes, round faces, and skin the color of coffee with double cream. Me, I'm more like a Hershey bar, and nothing about me is round or short. I've got lanky legs, long arms, high cheekbones, even long eyes. Mama calls me her "wee Watutsi woman."

Mama changed out of her nurse's aide uniform and into her jeans and cut-off purple sweatshirt. She winked at me and whispered, "Good thing our pioneer hearth is gas powered."

I laughed and said, "Good thing." Suddenly I was ashamed I even thought Super-Duper Stupid before, but that's how it is with thoughts. They're like uninvited guests, some of them, just popping in.

I told her about the essay contest. She hugged me fierce and said that she'd switch days if she had to so that she could come to my Awards Day. Just make sure to remind her as the time got closer, she said, so she could make the arrangements.

It wasn't exactly how I was planning on telling her, but it was nice enough.

She asked, "You have a copy of your prize-winning words?"

"A scrap copy," I said.

"Good enough," she answered.

I ran back and snatched it off my bed, where I'd left it when the meter man came.

She wiped her hands and sat at the table. I watched her read. She bit her lip and shook her head and sighed and smiled. I could tell she liked it. Then her eyes got all teary and it dawned on me. I should have remembered to cross out that part, but it was too late now. I knew the sentence that was in her eyes, the one that said, *And if I could follow my dreams, I'd follow them right to my daddy's doorstep and ask him if he ever had any dreams about coming back home and what are the chances that they'd ever come true.*

I held my breath. The tears went back behind Mama's eyes; they never did spill over her cheeks. She finished up with another sigh and a click of her tongue and said, "Janelle, one thing you don't need to dream anymore about is becoming a writer someday. You already are one."

She had that distant look like she gets when memories sneak up on her. I guessed she was probably remembering her own essay-and-poetry-contest days. Mama never told us about them, but Aunt Barbara did. She said Mama could write circles around most modern-day authors, but Mama just laughed and said, "Too late for that now. Real families need real food. That's why I have a real job."

TWO

We ate hamburgers on white bread slices. Mama called it buffalo steaks and cornbread, seeing that we were pioneers.

When we were through, I said, "Mama, I'll take the dishes to the stream and wash them in the waterfall." Talk about getting into the spirit!

"Janelle, you got some imagination!" Crystal said.

That sure made me smile. It made Mama smile, too, because she knew where my imagination came from.

Soon after supper, Aunt Barbara came knocking. Roxann yelled, "Who is it?" through the door like I should have done earlier in the day.

As soon as Roxann knew the caller, she shouted, "Aunt Barbara! Aunt Barbara! We're pioneers!" before our aunt's feet were even on our carpet. Aunt Barbara lived in our same apartment building, two floors up.

Aunt Barbara saw the candles. "Your power been shut off again?"

Mama nodded and said, "We'll get through."

Crystal said, "Pioneers didn't have TV anyway, Aunt Barbara," like that was the most important thing.

Mama said to Aunt Barbara, "Before you go, take the milk and the Muenster cheese, or they'll spoil." The refrigerator ran on electricity too.

"You got enough?" Aunt Barbara worried.

"A whole box of powdered milk in the cupboard for such emergencies," Mama said.

In our family, we didn't eat out at restaurants and we never got extras like fruit bits and ice cream and potato chips. There were days in a row when we all ate peanut-butter-and-jelly sandwiches for breakfast and supper and thanked our stars for free lunch at school in between. Lots of kids wrinkled up their noses about school food. Not us.

Mama always said that no matter what is or isn't under it, the most important thing is to keep your roof, meaning that rent was the most important bill.

I wondered if she ever thought that the most

important thing was keeping a whole family together, daddy and all, but I didn't ask. Didn't
dare. She'd wince and get that hurting look in
her eyes every time we said Daddy's name, almost like somebody stabbed her.

Maybe someday when some more time went
by, I'd bring up the question, but not now. Even
though she always told us we could talk about
anything anytime, I figured that Mama needed
time for sorting out and not explaining.

Funny thing was, I knew how she felt. I hated
it when Crystal and Roxann got to mentioning
Daddy. Bad enough he'd be in the back of my
mind. Then they'd say his name and he'd take
front and center and block out everything else.

I had real yo-yo feelings about Daddy, too. Up,
down. Angry, sad. Hurt, confused. Probably better
to just let it ride till it evened out some.

Aunt Barbara smiled at Mama and said, "Girl,
you oughta write it down." Here she goes again,
I thought.

"Write what down?" Mama asked, rolling her
eyes as usual.

"All of it. Everything you go through. Folks'd
love to hear your stories," said my aunt.

She's Mama's sister. They look like twins, like
Roxann and Crystal do, except for their styles,
which make them night and day.

Mama's sporty, with short cropped hair. Aunt Barbara lets her hair free and loose like a big, unpruned bush. She wears billowy clothes in vibrant colors, Africa hues she calls them, and jewelry that always leaves behind a wind-chime tinkle in my ears.

"Ha!" Mama waved her hand in a shooing gesture.

"Ha!" Aunt Barbara cut Mama off. She imitated her, waving her hand the exact same way. "I know, I know; real families need real food and that whole bit. That's a lame excuse if ever I heard one! You do your writing on the side."

"I've never been to college," Mama said. "You can't be a writer with no education."

Aunt Barbara laughed. "No education? You got knowledge they don't teach in any college."

"Listen to that poetry, will you?" Mama joked.

Aunt Barbara ignored her. "Heck, you'd be doing the world a favor, teaching a course in survival, in spite of what you say."

Aunt Barbara was still standing. Mama too. She motioned to the chairs, and they both sat down. The candlelight made wavy patterns on their faces and monster shapes on the wall.

I washed the dishes slow, to listen. Too many times Mama said, "Girls, let us grown-ups

be," and we'd have to find other things to oc-
cupy us.

"Who'd want to read about struggling anyway?" Mama asked. "Seems to me folks got
enough of that in their own lives."

"Ain't the struggling that's interesting," Aunt
Barbara said. "It's the way you pull it off."

"Well," said Mama, "I've really got no time
for such dribbling and scribbling."

"You oughta make time," Aunt Barbara insisted. "I'm telling you, girl. You oughta write it
down."

"We'll just leave the pulling off the struggle to
me and the writing to the writers, like Janelle
here." She nodded my way and told Aunt Barbara all about my essay award.

I thought Aunt Barbara's mouth would crack
from smiling and our floor from her jumping up
and down and my ribs from all her hugging. She
cried, too, when she read my winning entry.

She finally calmed down. Then she and Mama
chatted about hospital business where Mama
worked and about library business because Aunt
Barbara worked there. I joined my sisters in our
bedroom.

They were playing house. "Shh. Freeze. Don't
make a sound. It's the 'lectric man," Roxann
was saying to her dolly.

Aunt Barbara has a favorite saying for that: "A child learns what he lives." She said it's from a poem. I sure didn't have to figure that one out in my mind. I felt it in my heart, and it made me sad.

I got to wondering why Aunt Barbara wasn't a writer herself.

I stayed up doing my homework long after I could hear my sisters' sound-asleep breathing. The candle flame made the words flicker over the pages, so my reading went slower. My worries kept the drowsiness away. I wished I had some answers, wished that there was something I could do.

I finished my social studies and put the day into my journal. I looked at the entry. It wasn't just a collection of words. It was happiness, sadness, and worry. It wasn't simply sentences for folks to read. It was living, breathing life for folks to feel.

When I finally blew the candle flame out, a trail of smoke curled up. It seemed like it wrote a message in cursive in the black night air like sparklers do on the Fourth of July.

I squinted to see the words: *Girl, you oughta write it down,* it said. Was I dreaming? Soon as I blinked, the words were gone. I sniffed their smell and inhaled extra hard, and then I knew they hadn't really disappeared. They had taken on a different dimension and burned right into my brain.

Aunt Barbara's message wasn't meant just for Mama. All of a sudden, I knew it was meant for me!

THREE

Two days later, Friday, Mama got her pay-check. She cashed it at her lunch hour and got the electric turned back on. Crystal and Roxann were in a glorious state because they could watch all their favorite television programs after all. Friday was their stay-up night.

During the wee hours, Roxann woke up sick, throwing up and burning with fever. Mama slept curled on one end of the couch and Roxann on the other with a pot for when she started gagging.

Mama couldn't get a thing to stay down her. Not liquid painkiller, not cherry Kool-Aid, not even a sucked ice cube. Roxann's tummy kept tossing it right back up.

Crystal slept through, but I heard it and came

out every time. Mama kept saying, "Janelle, go back to sleep. No sense in three of us getting worn down."

Worn down was what Mama got for sure. By the time dawn came, she was frazzled with worry.

"Girls, get moving," she called at eight-thirty. "No time for breakfast today."

Not that I was hungry anyway, thinking about what was the matter with Roxann. I had other feelings for other needs besides breakfast, like wishing we had a car to drive in or a phone to call on. Or a daddy to make us feel more at ease. Especially a daddy. Our own daddy.

Once I told that to Aunt Barbara and she said, "There are all kinds of hunger, not always in the belly." I didn't understand it then. It sure made sense now, though, seeing as how I was hungering for Daddy more than food, even on an empty stomach.

"Good thing the doctor has Saturday morning office hours," Mama said, wrapping Roxann in a cozy afghan because she was shaking so hard off and on from the chills, even though the Indian summer sun was already shining warm and gold.

"How are you gonna pay?" I asked Mama.

"You let me do the worrying over money," she said. "I've paid part of the bill from last time already. And I pay a little bit every month."

I leaned back in my seat. Mama had a way of making me feel safe even when there was nothing to feel safe about.

We jostled on the bus the whole fourteen blocks. I thought sure Roxann's tummy would toss again, but she just slept across Mama's lap.

Mama signed in Roxann's name and waited at the reception window. The reception lady opened it. "Do you have an appointment?" she said.

"No, ma'am," said Mama.

"We'd really appreciate it if you'd call first in the future," the lady said, as if Mama had coleslaw in her head instead of brains.

"I'd be happy to call ahead if I had a phone to call on," Mama answered.

"Please be seated," the reception lady said. Good thing, because Roxann was weighing heavy in Mama's arms.

Next thing we knew, the reception lady was calling Mama's name. Mama went back up to the window. She put Roxann in my lap first.

A woman with a newborn baby smiled at us.

"My sister, she's burning up," said Crystal.

"I hope she feels better soon," the new mother said.

There was also a dad with a toddler in an arm cast and two more mothers with two kids apiece and one with three little blond-haired boys.

I looked up at the reception window. The lady was leaning forward, whispering something secret to Mama. Mama was leaning forward to hear.

All of a sudden, Mama's cocoa brown cheeks turned sun-fire red, and she was standing straight and tall. In a steady voice she said, "The bill will be paid eventually, like it always is. Meanwhile, this child is sick, and it's not her fault I still owe some money."

Part of me thought, Mama, be quiet; all these folks are listening and watching. The other part of me was cheering her on.

The reception lady whispered something else. I could see her pleading with her hands, probably trying to shut Mama up. Because right away Mama said, "There's no need for whispering. Now, you may have a new policy, but I got a policy too. We came all the way across town for one purpose, and we are staying put until the doctor sees Roxann." She was wearing her fiercest don't-mess-with-me look.

The reception lady whispered again. Her face was redder than Mama's. Mama nodded and sat down again, sliding Roxann easy back onto her lap. She looked straighter and taller than ever to me, even in her chair.

The new mother said, "You have a lovely family." I could tell that her eyes were full of admiration.

Mama looked at all of us. "Thank you. That I do," she said.

Mama asked the new mother about her baby, a boy named Marcus who had made his entrance just three weeks before. They sat there, engaging in that women-bonding conversation that turns strangers into instant friends.

Next thing we knew, it was Roxann's turn.

Mama heaved her onto her shoulder and carried her in. Crystal and I sat in the waiting room.

"They always take the really sick kids first," Crystal said.

"Uh-huh," the new mother said.

I knew they probably just wanted to get rid of Mama, but I didn't tell that to the new mother because she probably already knew. She was on Mama's side for sure. I had been watching her. I could tell by the look in her face every time she glanced in Mama's direction.

Mama and Roxann came back out a short time later with medicine. "Good thing we brought her," Mama said. "It's strep throat making her so ill." Roxann was so ill she said nothing.

Mama started walking out, with us following. "Psst," the new mother said. We all turned around.

"Go get 'em," she whispered, making a thumbs-up sign like you do to winners.

Mama made the sign back to her. So did Crystal. "I will" tumbled out of my mouth before I even realized I was speaking. Roxann just lolled on Mama's shoulder.

Being so tired, I started lolling too. Then I remembered that the library was on this very bus route. I bolted up. "Mama," I asked, "can I go visit Aunt Barbara?"

"Don't see any harm in that," said Mama. "She works until one. Just make sure you come home with her." It was ten after ten.

"I will, Mama," I said.

"You're not gonna get restless all that time?" she worried.

"Not me, Mama," I promised. I had plans, burning plans. Plans that kept the restlessness away.

"I'm hungry," Crystal groaned.

"Oh yeah; we haven't had breakfast yet," Mama remembered.

"I can wait for lunch. Really, Mama," I said when her eyebrows asked, *Are you sure?*

"Okay, then." She reached into her pocket and pulled out some change. "Here's your bus fare. Don't let Aunt Barbara pay."

FOUR

Aunt Barbara was happy to see me. Surprised, too, that I was all alone. I explained about Roxann.

Aunt Barbara had to run the preschool story hour at ten-thirty. Before she gathered all the children together, I asked her for some paper and a pencil.

"School project?" she asked, handing me the supplies.

"Report," I said, so I wouldn't be lying.

I wasn't quite ready to tell her yet, even though she's the one planted the seed, made the message burn into my brain. I decided to say nothing to nobody till I found out if my plan would work.

"Aunt Barbara," I asked, "why aren't *you* a

writer? You have such good ideas, and you're always around books and everything."

Aunt Barbara began ticking off on her fingers. "And I don't have the discipline. And I love reading better than writing. And my talents lie elsewhere."

I thought of her fantastic paintings and weavings. "Yeah, I guess you're an artist instead." She smiled.

Right then a man with a little girl came up and asked where the bird books were. My heart felt like it had jumped into my throat and wouldn't go down no matter how hard I swallowed. Seeing that man and that little girl together made me remember how it was with Daddy. That man was long and lean and three shades lighter than his little girl and she wore her hair in a fuzzy knob on the top, just like I did when I was in kindergarten. The way they held hands and smiled at each other made my whole self well up with feelings, sad and mad.

If things were different, it might be me with my own daddy here. Matter of fact, if things were different, I wouldn't even need to be here, trying to figure out how to write things down.

Aunt Barbara led them to the nature shelves. They all looked blurry to me as they walked over. I blinked, hard, before anyone saw. Then I

26

took a deep breath and said the Pledge of Allegiance in my head to keep the tears away. It was the first thing I could think of.

Aunt Barbara came back and said, "Sorry for the interruption. Now where were we?"

"I'm gonna write it down, just like you said," I blurted before I could stop myself. "I mean, I'm gonna try to be an author. My mind is burning with things to say."

Aunt Barbara gasped like she had swallowed a mosquito. "Really, child?"

"Yep," I said.

"Well, then, hang on a second." She flew to the reference-book shelf. She returned in a flash and thrust a book at me. "Here. This is what you need to get started."

The story-hour bell rang and all the little ones lined up. "Gotta go," she said, disappearing into a sea of toddlers.

Aunt Barbara liked to say, "You are what you believe yourself to be."

So I figured I'd best get to believing I was an honest-to-goodness writer so I'd be one. "You're a writer," I whispered to myself for the first time. Having Aunt Barbara believe it was double the force.

I sat in the children's section. It was quiet there now. I opened the book Aunt Barbara had given me. It was an all-about-writing book for beginners. At first it scared me. Plain overwhelmed me, the size of it alone. I thought, I'll never get through this. Where do I begin? Maybe I should just forget it.

Then I got a grip on myself and took a deep breath. I decided to do what Mama does with the Bible every night. I closed my eyes and just opened it at random. Mama says, "Don't have too much time for reading. This way, I get a daily smattering of spirituality."

Maybe if I got bits and pieces like that, little by little, it wouldn't be as scary as tackling it from cover to cover.

First thing my fingers found was an interview with a mystery writer. He said that before he even dared to write mysteries—and that's how he put it, *dared*—he read voraciously. I had to make a trip to the big dictionary for that one.

I found *voracious*. "Greedy," it said. "Too eager; insatiable; ravenous."

I looked up those words too. *Insatiable* meant "never satisfied," and *ravenous* meant "extremely hungry." I wondered if that meaning had anything to do with ravens. I'd have to find out.

Then two other thoughts popped into my head: Good thing I read a lot, and I'd better start reading even more.

I random-page-picked again. This time a woman author of children's books said, "Write what you know. Write what interests *you*. Chances are, it will interest a million other readers too."

I suddenly felt discouraged. What did I know? How to be poor? How to feel confused when your parents split up? Then I remembered. "Write it down," Aunt Barbara had kept telling Mama. Now here was a famous writer telling *me* the same thing!

"I will," I said, right out loud.

Two of the mothers who were waiting for their story-hour toddlers smiled at me. I felt my cheeks get hot and was glad I was so dark because maybe the blush wouldn't show on me like it does on Roxann and Crystal.

I buried my face in that book deep as I could, and then the story-room door opened, so I was saved. The mothers went over to meet their little ones. The little ones all had lunch-bag puppets in their hands.

Aunt Barbara looked my way and made a "whew" sign like she was wiping her brow. I smiled at her and looked at the clock. 11:03. I still had almost two hours.

I read an article about the things editors look for in good writing. Then I copied names of editors and addresses from magazines. I actually pictured editors opening my letters and reading my manuscripts. That's what pieces of unpublished writing are called—manuscripts.

I nearly laughed out loud at the thought. I was getting ahead of myself, way ahead. I didn't even have a manuscript yet!

"Janelle."

I jumped.

"Listen. We've got a problem, niece," Aunt Barbara said. "You remember Ophelia?"

I nodded. Ophelia was Aunt Barbara's coworker with straight blond hair who always wore cat pins on her clothes.

"She just went home sick with the flu, and it's Jack's day off, so I'm going to have to work till five. Now what am I going to do about getting you home?"

My face lit up. "Good. I'm glad, Aunt Barbara. That's no problem to me."

She cocked her head.

"I mean, I'm not glad Ophelia's sick or anything," I said. "It's just that I'd rather be here than almost anywhere right now."

"But what about lunch?" Aunt Barbara worried. "I won't even get to think about lunch today. Saturdays are frantic as it is, let alone with two of us gone."

"That's no problem to me," I repeated. "I'm not hungry, Aunt Barbara, not for lunch." I was thinking about the dictionary. "I'm just ravenous for words."

Her eyebrows went up and she said, "That so? Well, you just solved both my problems. I'll go call Mr. Bruno on my floor. I'm sure he'd be happy to go down and tell your mama why you'll be late."

FIVE

Aunt Barbara left me alone.

I don't know where the hours went, vanished like a breath of kettle steam in the kitchen air. I only knew it was closing time because the lights all dimmed.

I had found out lots before closing time, but not enough. I looked around for a hiding place for my book to safeguard it for next time. I hid it behind the huge philodendron plant up high on the holiday-books shelf. I knew the plant was a philodendron because all the plants have labels, which is a pretty good idea for a library.

"Have you gobbled enough words yet?" Aunt Barbara's voice came out of nowhere.

"Aunt Barbara, you scared me half to death!" I hissed.

She jerked her head toward the philodendron and the book. "Well?"

"Well. Uh. Um," I started spurting. "You can't check out reference books and, uh . . ."

Aunt Barbara laughed and slid the book out from behind the plant. "Right you are," she said. "Patrons can't, but librarians can borrow them overnight. And you're in luck with an extra day at that, 'cause who's going to miss it when we're closed on Sunday? Certainly not Mr. Phil O. Dendron here." She tucked it under her arm.

"Aunt Barbara, thanks!" I yelped, then cupped my hand over my mouth. Luckily most folks had already cleared out.

"Want some real supper?" Aunt Barbara asked as I got my jacket from the chair. "Woman can't live on words alone, you know."

"Sure, but Mama will wonder . . ."

"Already put that part into the message when I called Mr. Bruno. Told him to tell her we were dining out tonight."

"Thanks, Aunt Barbara. You're too much," I said.

"Well, we editors like to keep our writers happy." She handed me the book. I waited in the foyer while she disappeared into the employees' room. She swished back out in a long fringed cape, swirled with every color of the rainbow.

"That is," she continued as if she had never paused, "you'd do me the honor of showing me your work first."

"Aunt Barbara, I wouldn't have anyone else for my editor."

She called "good night" to the maintenance man and put her arm around me. We walked out. The blast of cold air hit us like a slap.

Aunt Barbara clutched her cape collar. "Holeee!" she exclaimed. "Where's all that golden Indian summer heat?"

"Beats me."

"That's living on Lake Erie for you," Aunt Barbara said. "Only place on this continent, I'll bet, where four seasons can happen all in one day."

I pulled my jacket zipper up to my chin and hugged the book with all my might.

We took the bus three blocks to the Bob Evans Restaurant. Aunt Barbara says their fresh-baked biscuits alone are worth coming for.

I didn't realize how hungry I was till the hostess seated us and I smelled all that food.

"How do you feel now?" Aunt Barbara asked, rubbing her icy hands.

"Hung—" I began. "Ravenous, absolutely ravenous."

"Good." Aunt Barbara nodded.

The waitress came. "We'll have hot cocoa and a basketful of biscuits, just for starters," she said.

SIX

The temperature stayed cold, so I spent all day Sunday on my bed with that book. Would have anyway, even if the weather had been rope-skipping perfect.

My best friend, Babs Wilson, and second-best friends, Linda Kalenda and Veronica de la Fuente, came knocking. Wanted to play Scrabble Junior with me.

We started a game, but I kept taking too long, they said. I'd see a word, and I started seeing sentences, thinking up phrases for the story I was going to write. My mind kept wandering off in a daydream. They got annoyed with me and left. I didn't even try to stop them.

By Thursday, my head was spinning from every how-to-write item and all the hints from editors and writers. Aunt Barbara had brought that book home every evening and returned it next morning when she went to work.

So on Thursday night, after math homework, I started my first story and gave it to Aunt Barbara, who gave me a few suggestions.

I wrote and wrote till my story had a satisfying feeling. Some of her suggestions I used; others, I didn't. Aunt Barbara said that was fine. "I'm only an editor, not the Divine Being. *You're* the writer."

I got like a fire raging out of control. My first idea was the match. Once that was struck, the flames kept catching.

The idea for my story came easy because I was living it. I wrote about true stuff going on each day, like the doctor visit with Roxann, with a few exaggerations, I'll admit, to give it spice.

"Nothing wrong with taking a little license," Aunt Barbara said when I worried that it wasn't a hundred percent true. "Realistic fiction, that's what you're giving the world."

A lot came out of my journal, tiny bits and pieces I'd never have recalled if I hadn't written them down.

Aunt Barbara let me use the typewriter at the library as well as her own at her apartment. That was the hard part.

"Why can't I just print neatly?" I complained.

"After all, President Lincoln wrote the Gettysburg Address on a paper bag." We had learned that at school.

" 'Cause you ain't Lincoln, and this ain't Gettysburg," she said with a sigh. "Now practice up."

She was right. Just when I was about to give up, my fingers took to those keys like they were born doing it.

"Necessity is the mother of invention," Aunt Barbara said. I'd heard that quote before. It's Benjamin Franklin, I think.

Of course, Wite-Out and I became best friends. Writing was harder work than I thought. Not to mention expensive. That's right, downright expensive.

The how-to book said that every time you send out a story, you have to send an SASE, a self-addressed stamped envelope, or you won't get an answer. Especially you won't get your manuscript back if they decide not to print it. That made me nervous, thinking of my stories in somebody's office. Maybe they just tossed them out, but who knows? Maybe they passed them around and got ideas of their own. I'd send an SASE for sure, every time.

One night in mid-November, Mama asked all of us what we wanted for Christmas.

"Stamps," I said quickly.

"Me too," Roxann squealed. "I want a Winnie-the-Pooh stamp and a Barney Dinosaur stamp."

"I saw a whole holiday pack," Crystal interrupted. "There was a Valentine's heart and a Christmas angel, things like that, plus a three-colored ink pad to go with it."

"I guess that's all the rage these days," said Mama. "What happened to stickers?"

"I want stickers, too," Roxann pleaded.

"Thought so." Mama laughed. She marked her list and looked up.

"Anything else, Janelle?"

"I was talking about mailing stamps," I said. "You know, for letters?"

"You mean for manuscripts." Mama understood. She knew what I was doing.

"And as long as you asked," I continued, "I wouldn't mind some typing paper and envelopes."

"I ain't never heard of elves makin' mailin' stamps and givin' out things like typing paper and envelopes," Roxann said. "What kinda presents are those?"

"They're called practical gifts," I told her.

"What's that mean?" she asked.

"Things you *need*, not just *want*," I explained.

Roxann frowned. "Santa only brings fun presents. He don't bring no practical gifts."

"Does so," Crystal chimed in. "Santa brings all kinds of gifts, even if they *aren't* fun."

"Uh-uh," Roxann insisted.

Mama winked at me and I shrugged. My sisters were still arguing over Santa and his choice of gifts when Aunt Barbara came knocking.

"I'm here to invite you all to Thanksgiving dinner next week," she said.

"Next week already?" Mama cried. "Girl, I never even gave it a thought."

"Well, now you don't have to. I'll go out and buy a big fat turkey and all the fixings and I'll do us a dinner, long as I get help with the dishes."

"You got yourself a deal, sister," Mama said, hugging Aunt Barbara hard.

"Deal," we all sang, making it a group hug.

SEVEN

Mama said the Thanksgiving prayer. When she got to the part about giving thanks for being together, her voice got Jell-O jiggly.

"Amen," Aunt Barbara said quickly, and a second later spoons and plates were clinking together and Mama and Aunt Barbara were laughing like old times.

My stomach clenched into an angry knot. Daddy always said the prayer. It was our tradition. Remembering made the knot grow tighter. Where was he eating dinner? Was he thinking of us today? What kind of prayer was he saying? Did he remember last year how he saved the wishbone for Roxann because she'd never broken one yet and how he'd pretended that she had won the bigger piece?

" 'Scuse me," I said, heading for the bathroom.

Mama pushed back her chair, but Aunt Barbara put a hand on her arm to stop her. Good thing. I needed a minute alone. Some time to let it all out.

The tears came like a downpour, sudden and quick. Then I gulped hard and it was over. I turned on the tap and splashed water, cold as I could get it, on my eyes. Aunt Barbara's towel rack is right above the heater vent, so drying my face felt warm and good.

My stomach unwound and I dished up my dinner till I was overfull like everyone else.

Crystal and I shared dish duty while Roxann fell asleep.

Late that night at home, when my sisters were asleep and I wasn't, Mama poked her head in. "I know. I miss him too" was all she said. She left before I could ask her to pull the wishbone with me. Her face was wet and shiny.

It was like she had been reading my mind and the story I was writing all at once. "Thanksgiving Tears" was the title.

I put down my pad and pencil and picked up the wishbone. I turned it over and over in my hands, wondering if you could just wish on it before it's broken and you get the bigger piece. I decided it was worth a try. So I clasped it and sunk into my pillow, wishing with all my might.

Fell asleep wishing too, because when I woke up, I was holding the bigger piece in my hand. The smaller one was lost somewhere in my sheets.

EIGHT

*C*hristmas vacation began with a bang. The first big blowout I ever had with my friends, that is.

"Don't you ever do anything else?" Babs asked one day when they all came over and found me writing—again.

"Yeah," I said, "when I have time."

"And when's that?" Linda asked.

"When I'm not writing," I said stupidly.

"Which is absolutely never," Veronica said.

"You can say that again," Babs agreed.

"Boy, you guys are starting to sound like my sisters instead of my friends," I said.

"Out of the mouths of babes, as they say. Maybe younger people have a point after all," said Babs.

"And it might not hurt you to listen," Veronica added.

I was fuming. My fists clenched and I could feel my jaw tighten too. How dare they side with my sisters against me?

"Tell you what," Linda said. "Next time *you* want to do something or you need a friend, don't call me."

"Or me," chimed Babs and Veronica together.

"We could all move to Hawaii, and she'd never even know the difference," Babs added. "Let's go."

They left without saying good-bye.

I pushed the argument right out of my mind. Had to. I finally put the finishing touches on my first story and, with Aunt Barbara's input, sent out letters to four different magazines. I made sure to send my phone number and social security number like the how-to book said to do.

Aunt Barbara said, "Now the hard part begins."

"What're you talking about?" I was shocked. "I just got the hardest part out of the way."

"Wait till you see what waiting is like," she replied. "Now me, if I were a writer, I'd start a new project right away to keep my mind off the first. At least that's what all the writers I've met say is the best thing."

Then she mentioned my homework. I've got to admit I would have let it slack some. Good thing she got me back on track. All it took was mention of Awards Day to do it.

"Priorities, Janelle," she said. I hated that word, but I knew her message was right.

She also mentioned the fight with my friends.

"What, did Crystal and Roxann blab about that?" My teeth were gritting.

"Chill out, girl," Aunt Barbara said. "And never mind how I found out. But you know, whatever you write is worth a pile of nothing if you don't have an appreciative audience. Catch my drift?"

"But Aunt Barbara," I argued weakly, "they think I have time for everything."

"You do, Janelle," she said. "See, it's all about blending, niece. Too much black makes the world too dark. Too much white is downright blinding. As in all work and no play, get it?"

I gave her a You're-Right-and-Thanks-for-Not-Making-Me-Say-It look. "Okay, Aunt Barbara. I'll write them notes, soon as I get home."

Aunt Barbara shook her head and picked up the receiver. I had no choice. I hesitated. Felt like my arm was stuck to my side. She just shook it at me and came toward me, so I had to take it.

I called Babs's house first. Lucky break for me, Linda and Veronica were both there, so I connected with all three that very night. Only had to make a fool of myself once.

Apologies aren't my favorite thing. I tripped over my tongue a million times. Sure am glad nobody was taping me! I never thought anything that made me squirm so bad could make me feel so good.

Aunt Barbara pretended she was reading the newspaper, but I figured she'd been listening all along. Knew for sure when she peeked over the top and gave me an I'm-Proud-of-You glance on my way out.

I worked on rescheduling my life. Kept my schoolwork up and wrote like a demon. Most important, Babs and Linda and Veronica and I were a foursome again.

Gray is beautiful, I thought.

NINE

Aunt Barbara was right about waiting. I waited and waited, seemed like a whole year long. I even wrote two more stories like she said and kept up my journal, aside from everything else I had to do, now that I was blending it all together.

Nothing took my mind off that first story, though. Some days I thought I'd die of waiting. Just flat-out die.

Then finally I came home from school one day and there was the mail. Not just any mail.

The envelope with my very own name on it flapped like a broken-winged bird from all the shaking my hands were doing. I opened it carefully, bit by little bit. All that believing paid off because here was a letter from one of the magazines I'd mailed to, telling me I was a writer and paying me to be one.

I turned the check this way and that. I set it down on the table so it would be still when I read it. It *did* say two hundred dollars! I would have fainted, except I was so happy, I didn't want to miss a second of the feeling.

My heart thudded extra. Those butterflies were swarming again, fluttering frantic.

I heard Mama and my sisters coming up the steps.

I tried acting normal when they walked in. Mama said, "How are you, Janelle?"

Good thing people can't hear your heartbeats when they start going crazy. All I could think of was African talking drums. My heartbeats sounded more like screaming drums.

I said, "Just fine," so nonchalant it almost convinced me.

She said, "Any mail?"

I said, "Yeah, some coupons on the counter."

"Good, no bills," she said, taking off her cape.

"And this." I handed her the check.

"Janelle, what is this?" Mama turned the check over, same as I had, as if the back was going to show her something.

"Janelle?" Her voice was like a siren.

Crystal and Roxann came running. "What?" "Can I see?"

"It's a check for two hundred dollars," Mama announced, "made out in your big sister's name."

She turned to me. "Janelle, what's it for?"

"For writing it down, just like Aunt Barbara said."

I told about my story and how I had sent it to the magazine. Now they were believing I was a writer, I could tell, because they all stood staring for a minute like they had never laid eyes on me before. Staring like I'd just dropped in from Jupiter.

Suddenly Mama threw back her head and yelped with joy and we all hugged and jumped and danced around like Masai folks having a celebration.

"Mama," I panted. "Can I go tell Aunt Barbara?"

"Absolutely!" Mama shouted. I rocked back and forth while she counted out my bus fare. I took the letter but handed the check to Mama. "You better hold this."

"Go!" she said, after looking at the time. "If you run, you can catch the five-fifteen. Be home before dark."

I dashed out and made the bus with a minute to spare.

Aunt Barbara was on her dinner break when I got there, wouldn't you just know it? She was working till nine tonight. I went back out and waited patiently as I could on the marble steps.

She spotted me as she came up the walk. "Something wrong, Janelle?" she asked.

"No! Something's right!" I said. "Here." She read the letter I shoved into her hands.

"Janelle! Janelle!" she shrieked. Suddenly I was being smothered in flowing embroidered muslin and bushy hair, and I couldn't tell whether Aunt Barbara was laughing or crying. I don't think she knew either. Don't think she cared. I know I didn't.

She made a big deal out of me to all her coworkers, saying "my niece the writer" every chance she got.

When it was time to go, I danced out the library door and up the bus's steps.

My heart was still dancing when I went to sleep. My mind was dreaming up other stories that my fingers were itching to write.

Even the thought of Daddy not being there couldn't make me sad tonight. Uh-uh. Made me happy instead, thinking somehow that he knew, that somehow he caught some of our excitement through the air and was lying somewhere at this very minute, smiling too.

TEN

I wasn't rich. I only felt like I was, and if that's believing, then it's the same thing.

Mama helped me cash my check the next day. I said, "Let's all get dressed elegant and go out for dinner."

"Janelle," Mama said, "it's *your* money. Do something *you* really want to do."

"Mama, money's no good unless it's shared," I told her. "That's what I want to do."

"That's wonderful of you," she said. "Then share it, but why not spend it on something that'll last a little longer than a solitary meal?"

She was talking sense. "Okay," I said.

I decided to take us all shoe shopping. We each got a pair of dressy shoes. Crystal's were navy. Roxann's were blue and white. Mine and Mama's were just plain black. They only cost fifty-one dollars and eighty-four cents with the tax, so I was still fixed.

I went to The Earring Boutique in the same plaza as the shoe store and found long, dangly, silver alphabet earrings that I knew would put a twinkle in Aunt Barbara's eye when I gave them to her.

I offered to buy us dinner at Burger King. "Okay," said Mama, "I'll go along with that."

"I'm asking Aunt Barbara," I said. "It's only right, since she was the one gave me the gift of that thought."

When I saw Aunt Barbara that night, she said, "Oh, Janelle, I'd love to, but I . . . I promised, uh, a coworker I'd work for her tonight." She stuttered and stammered her words. "How 'bout tomorrow night?"

The whole thing peeved me. What was more important than my dinner? And which coworker anyway? I knew all their names by now. How come she couldn't just say "Ophelia" or "Karen" or "Ysabel" like a normal person?

I didn't bother asking either, because I was so mad. Aunt Barbara walked me down to my door like everything was normal, and she and Mama talked after I went in and moped in my bedroom over changing my plans.

I tossed the earrings on my dresser and heard

them clink in the box. Now I had to wait even longer to give them to her, shoot!

Next night, I was excited instead of mad. As soon as I opened that Burger King door, there was Aunt Barbara wearing a lip-splitting smile, same as Babs, Veronica, and Linda. "Surprise!" they shouted.

I turned around and looked at Mama and my sisters. Their lips were in danger of ripping too. "You knew?" I asked.

"Yep," said Mama, "and can you believe even Roxann kept the secret?"

"Mama," I said, "if Roxann can keep a secret like that, anything's possible."

There was a shiny silver helium balloon. CONGRATULATIONS was printed on the front. TO OUR FAVORITE AUTHOR was written on the back.

Believing I was an author had made me one for sure! They all believed it too, not just me and my family. Knowing that made my head feel lighter than the balloon.

Only thing weighing down my balloon was that Daddy wasn't here to celebrate too. Nothing, even the real treats like this party, felt whole without him. I felt angry about him not being here, but I pushed the anger away for now best as I could. The thought of missing puzzle pieces kept poking at my brain again and again.

I paid for Mama's dinner and mine, my sisters' and Aunt Barbara's like I promised. But Aunt Barbara insisted on paying the rest. "I threw you the party, so don't argue with me," she said.

I didn't argue.

I gave her the earrings and she went wild over them just like I'd hoped.

The rest of the money we used for odds and ends—me, Mama, and my sisters.

We sure weren't rich, but it was a pleasure to be acquainted with Comfortable for a moment in time.

ELEVEN

Awards Day was another proud moment. I felt balloon high again. Now I had two trophies, except one was gold and one was in the form of words.

Crystal got three *A*'s on her report card and a "perfect attendance" certificate.

Roxann graduated from kindergarten wearing a miniature cap and gown like high schoolers get. Crystal and I went with Mama to the ceremony, which was held at night because most parents work days.

Summer started in the city, hot and heavy. We spent our time jumping rope, playing jacks, rap dancing, and getting drenched when the firemen opened the hydrant like a fountain. We slurped its sweet coolness and danced in its mist and watched the steam coming off our clothes for the rest of the afternoon.

I felt old and important that year. I was an author and a spelling-bee winner, and now I was a sister-sitter besides. Crystal and Roxann didn't need to go to the city center while Mama worked. She had decided I was old enough and responsible enough as well.

Sitting had its drawbacks, though. The more responsibilities I took on, the less time I had for writing things down. I got into a mode, though, and found I was writing inside my head almost every minute. The whole world started looking different to me now. There was a story in absolutely everything—and absolutely everyone.

Then Mama lost her job. I knew before she told me. That night her footsteps were slower, and she sunk right into the flower-print chair before even asking how all of us were, and where. She shook her head, and sobs shook her body. "What am I gonna do now?" she asked the thin air.

But I answered anyway. "We'll get through." Seemed like the natural thing to say. Couldn't think of anything else. Besides, we had no choice except to get through.

I felt like screaming "Daddy, where are you?

How come you're not helping?" Probably would have too if he were right in front of me. But then, if he were right in front of me, things wouldn't be so bad no matter what. And if they were, they wouldn't *seem* so.

I tried saying "We'll get through" again to Mama, but it came out quiet and quivery.

Mama pulled me onto her lap and rocked me like I was a baby again, and suddenly I was wishing I were.

"Livin' is such a seesaw, Janelle," Mama said. "First you're up feelin' almost like you're in the clouds."

I thought of the balloon-high feeling.

"Then," she continued, "you land with a bump that rattles right through to your soul."

I knew Mama was bumped bad and rattling hard. I leaned hard against her, knowing that love could stop it some and wishing that love could stop it all.

Comfortable was a feeling that had spread its wings and taken off like a bird gone south. I felt like winter. No song, no color, just bitter cold that made me ache. Bleak.

I tried calling Comfortable back, but I knew it wasn't coming till I set the scene. I knew it was up to me just like before. I'd been slacking. Now

I had half the summer long. Time to pick up my pace. Time to pick up my pencil.

When you have dreams, you don't expect them to have nightmare endings. I wrote and wrote. I scribbled poems and stories, mostly stories.

The day my first envelope came back, I ripped it open, knowing another publisher would like my story, believing there was another check.

My manuscript came back, just as I sent it, with a little green slip tucked inside. "We regret that we do not see a place for your article in our publication at this time. Best of luck in placing it elsewhere," it said.

You know what I did? I ripped that little green slip so hard, ripped it into a thousand pieces. And then I cried tears, thousands of them.

It happened twice again. That's when I quit. Maybe I wasn't believing hard enough, but I was no writer, no way, no how.

Aunt Barbara asked one day, "Anything new on the publishing scene?"

I told her all about the nightmare endings to my dreams, and she said, "Course you got rejections. That's what writing is about. Even famous writers get them all the time. I'm always getting magazines at work that feature authors and that's the thing they all have in common. It makes you better, makes you tougher. And those bitter rejections—they make the acceptances taste soooo sweet!"

My mouth almost watered. If I didn't trust Aunt Barbara and she didn't work at the library and know what the publishing world was about, I'd tell her to put that information in the deepest, trashiest landfill ever created. But because I did trust her more than almost any other living person, I decided to put her advice in my recycling bin. Of course I'm talking about a space in my mind. I had to save it. Couldn't use it right now. I'd been bumped, and I was rattling hard. Too hard to do anything but rock the bruises away.

TWELVE

The seesaw went up again. Mama and Roxann and Crystal and me, we were all in the clouds together.

My baby sisters and I knew something was up when we got up one gloomy morning and there was Mama, glowing like the sun itself.

"Your daddy will be here tonight," she said, "home to stay."

And we all hugged and jumped and danced around like those celebrating Masai people again.

Our questions ran wild like sheep let loose. Mama tried to lasso and tackle them one by one.

Our daddy had been gone a year now with no word. No word, we *thought*. All the while he and Mama had been sneaking phone calls through Aunt Barbara. Didn't want to disap-

61

point us with high hopes and no deeds, they decided. Didn't want to plant any seeds unless they could help them grow.

Now they made a new decision, a decision to try again. A decision that whatever happened—good or bad—it was better if it happened to all of us together.

"Does Daddy have a job?" Crystal asked.

"Did," Mama answered, "but now he's outa work again and lookin'. Had some possibilities, but they fell through."

Rejections, I thought. Daddy knew the feeling, just like me, and he's trying again. We were kindred spirits; I could feel it.

Oh, I had so much to tell him!

The morning dragged along, snail slow. By noon I thought the world had stopped dead on its axis.

Crystal said, "I'm goin' to sleep. It'll make the day go faster."

I thought Mama'd make ruts in the furniture from dusting over and over. "It's all clean," I told her.

"It's something to do, Janelle," she said, swiping the same spots.

And Roxann. I'm surprised she didn't suck her thumb clean off! She hadn't put it anywhere near her mouth since the week before kindergarten. Quit, just like that, saying, "I'm a big schoolgirl now."

Me, I paced like a pent-up circus tiger.

"Janelle," Mama said, "go take a walk or something, okay? Your jitters are givin' me the heebie-jeebies."

I went to Veronica's. "My dad's coming home tonight," I said.

"Whew!" Veronica whistled loud and shrill. "You mean it? No wonder you're restless as a chipmunk trapped in a station wagon."

That was Veronica's expression about anyone who was on edge, because once her aunt and uncle took her to Allegheny State Park and a chipmunk got in their car. Nearly went crazy till her uncle pulled over and opened the back.

"Here." Veronica pulled me to the kitchen table and pushed my shoulders down till I sat. "Start snapping."

I helped her with a big bowl of green beans, then we started to shell a smaller bowl of peas. Veronica's mother is big on fresh veggies, puts them into everything she cooks.

When we got done with the veggies, Veronica said, "Wanna play Guess Who?"

"Anything," I said.

Funny thing happened, though. The male characters all looked like Daddy—Joe, Alex,

Max, Robert, Herman—all of them, fat, thin, dark, or light. It didn't matter. I threw up my hands and they slapped on my knees. "It's hopeless," I said.

Veronica sighed, flipped the tabs, and put the game away. She went to her room and brought back two embroidery-thread friendship bracelets that were just started.

"Here. Braid," she ordered.

I finished my pink-and-blue one and got an idea. "Veronica, you have any extra thread?" I asked.

"A whole drawer." She stood up and I followed her to the dining room cabinet. She pulled it open.

"Wow!" I exclaimed. I took a black skein and a white and we went back to the kitchen.

"I need this one extra long," I said, measuring and cutting the threads.

Veronica frowned, then figured it out a second later. "I get it— a coming-home present for your dad."

"Uh-huh," I said through my teeth as I held the ends together with my mouth.

"Black and white. Good colors for a man." Veronica approved.

"Good colors for balance," I mumbled, thinking about seesaws and Aunt Barbara's gray.

I finished Daddy's bracelet and wrapped it in a paper towel. I pictured it burning a hole in my pocket, but it was more patient than me.

I stopped at Babs's and went home before suppertime. Mama's meat loaf smell made my belly churn. Meat loaf, Daddy's favorite.

"Wash up, Janelle," Mama called when she heard the door. Didn't even turn from the sink, where she was peeling the potatoes. "And then cut these up, will you? Crystal, please set the table."

Roxann sat on the couch, sucking her thumb in front of "Sesame Street." Crystal started saying, "Why can't Roxann . . ."

"Let her be," whispered Mama, just as quick.

I was on my way to the stove with a potful of cut potatoes when I heard the click of the doorknob. I jumped. Some water splashed out on the floor. I mopped it with a swish of my sock.

Crystal wasn't so lucky. She sent a plate shattering to the floor.

And Roxann, I was sure her thumb would go down in one gulp.

THIRTEEN

Paddy just stood in the doorway, staring like he maybe opened some stranger's door instead.

I breathed out the sigh that had been stuck in my chest since morning. Somehow I feared I might not recognize him after so long, but Aunt Barbara was right, She said, "The eyes are one thing, Janelle. They can play tricks on you. But the heart, well, that's another thing. When it snaps a picture, believe me, child, you never forget."

He was the same as I remembered, with a glow all around him that overflowed into the apartment.

Before I could blink, he and Mama were in each other's arms, laughing and rocking up a storm. Then he bear-hugged us all in turn, me first. Didn't say a word, just held on, swaying back and forth. Every now and then he'd hold me out to look at me, then he'd grab me fiercely back again. He smelled just like I remembered, too, a different kind of man smell that Mama, Aunt Barbara, Crystal, Roxann, and I didn't have. I took a long whiff when his grip let up a bit, and it gave me a memory of being teddy-bear-clutching, blanket-holding, tucked-into-bed safe.

I'd have to tell Aunt Barbara that the nose is just like the heart. It doesn't forget either.

Crystal shocked everyone by bursting like a rain cloud. Just sobbed and sobbed with huge wet tears, like a kindergarten jump roper who'd just scraped both knees. Mama called them dam-breaking tears. Said Crystal's feelings got so built up that they had to find an outlet somehow.

Roxann was worse than Crystal, only different. Clung to Mama like the time she was sick, only this time she had clinging strength.

And me with my great idea of having so much to tell my dad. I flat-out lost my tongue. Couldn't find it for the rest of that night no how. Just handed Daddy the bracelet silently.

That was all right, though, I figured. We had time now. The missing puzzle piece was back in its place. I allowed myself to just stand back a while, admiring its completeness.

Mostly I listened. Listened to him and Mama exchanging ideas and swapping promises. Watched them holding hands and stroking memories. Liking how my bracelet hugged his wrist.

Mama asked Daddy how he felt.

"Full up, for the first time in a whole long year," he answered. "Man, how I been hungering for my family!"

Aunt Barbara was right. There are all kinds of hunger, not always in the belly. Daddy felt it too.

And speaking of hunger, I'm glad Mama finally announced dinner. Because by then my stomach was taking over for my mouth, sounding like it was talking right out loud.

Daddy loved the meat loaf, saying over and over how it was the best thing he'd tasted since the last time he was home.

I enjoyed listening more than I ever thought I could. By dessert, Crystal was chattering again. The sounds of the dishes clinking, dishwater running, their voices—even Roxann's thumb sucking and baby monkey whimpering—gave me that snug sensation.

The tone of my house was perfect again. All this time, it had been like a staticky radio station. Now it was all cleared up, and I liked tuning in to the harmony.

That night I made a list of all the life riddles

I'd heard throughout my years. Some of them I didn't understand till I was living right in the middle of them. Lately I was doing a lot of living in the middle, feeling like a tornado had me captive right in its eye.

When I got too tired to write anymore, I said "hello" to the new stories visiting my head, greeted them nicely so they'd stay and feel right at home until I had a chance to write them down.

Oh, I thought. I have so much to write! Pencils, get ready. Here I come!

FOURTEEN

I heard it like that for the first week or two. Then, strange thing, seemed like the static returned, crackling worse than ever.

It's all so weird, I thought. Sometimes the people I expect ought to know best turn out to be the biggest strangers. Take Daddy, for example.

Here was the man I was part of, the person who gave me half of everything I was. Here was the man who had read to me, scolded me, punished me, fed me, comforted me, come to my school events when he could, and loved me for all of my life.

Then he left for one year and turned into someone else. Mama didn't act like it, but that's sure how it seemed to me, and I think my sisters too.

The worst part was how *we* all turned into someone else soon as he walked back into our lives. And I couldn't *see* what had changed as much as I *felt* it.

Roxann clung to Mama all the time now, reminding me of a baby orangutan. Her clinging to Mama and ignoring him made Daddy mad, which made Crystal come to his rescue and treat him like he was wearing a crown, which made me furious because I can't stand brownnosers, especially in families, which made Mama mad because she can't stand people being at odds, especially in families. We lived in a circle of annoyances. But something else was wrong, too.

Aunt Barbara didn't come down so often anymore. And when she did, she kept her visits short. When I asked her why, she said, "I hate to intrude," which got me mad all over again because I missed her and I missed the old times.

"You're not an intruder, Aunt Barbara; you're family!" I screamed. I stomped so hard that I shocked myself, besides hurting my foot.

She said, "It's different now, Janelle."

"You're telling me!" I yelled. "One of my sisters is a jealous little baby, the other is a daddy's girl, and my own mother has no time for me. I could win the Pulitzer Prize and you know what she'd probably do? She'd probably say, 'Oh, how nice,' and ask my father what he wanted for supper that night."

The anger welled up from deep inside me somewhere and spilled from my mouth. Once it started, I couldn't stop it. It gushed like a broken faucet. I paced and spluttered till I was out of breath.

"It was supposed to be great having him back. It was supposed to make everything right again. And instead of being orderly and fine like it's supposed to be, it's all helter-skelter and turned upside down."

Suddenly I fizzled out, like a car run out of gas.

Aunt Barbara was staring at me. I looked at the floor. I felt my cheeks grow hotter by the second. I knew I'd done it now, proved myself as a spoiled selfish brat who couldn't keep her wishes straight, who wanted a daddy when he was gone and wanted him gone when he was home.

I turned to leave. Aunt Barbara grabbed my arm. "You in a hurry?" she asked.

"Yes," I said. "No."

"I hope not," she said, "because I could use some company. To tell you the truth, I sure miss the long night visits too."

I hugged her then. The sobs were bubbling just below the surface like a volcano. Just as they were about to erupt, my hair got tangled in her earring. We both started laughing and untangling ourselves.

"The alphabets," I noticed.

"My favorites," she said.

I was glad.

"You know," she told me, "whether good or bad, stress is stress, and it always makes a mess."

"Aunt Barbara, there you go again with your poetry. You *are* a writer!" I exclaimed. "But what is good stress?" That sure sounded like a contradiction if I ever heard one!

"Getting married, landing a better job, moving." She gave a few examples.

"Or getting a family all back together," I added.

"Exactly," she said. "You know, Janelle, all the things great stories are made of." She had a twinkle in her eye.

"Gotcha," I said, giving her the thumbs-up sign.

"I'd say that this calls for a double-chocolate, double-scoop, rolled-in-sprinkles sugar cone," she announced.

The writer in me already had the first paragraph of a Daddy-makes-a-difference story dying to get on paper. But my sweet tooth would never forgive me. Nor my longing for the good old times with my one-in-a-million relative.

I walked to Friendly's with Aunt Barbara. We

oohed and aahed like old times over our double-chocolate, double-scoop, rolled-in-sprinkles sugar cones.

"Aunt Barbara," I said, "do you think things are really changed that much?"

"What do you think?" she asked me back, sucking runny chocolate out the pointed end of her cone.

I took a munch of my cone and just smiled at her. I never did answer. I didn't have to.

When I got home, I found Daddy sitting on the edge of my bed, thumbing through my latest nature magazine. He tapped the page with the Canada goose article.

"Now here's somethin'," he said. "These geese keep the same partners all through their lives."

"Uh-huh," I said, wondering why he was suddenly interested in Canada geese.

"Betcha this mom and these goslings would get into a ruffle if he just took off, then flew back to the nest and settled back in like he belonged there all the while. Wouldn't blame them a bit if there was some squawkin' and feathers flyin'." He tapped the picture again and closed the magazine.

I looked down and clammed up. That tongue of mine sure had a way of tying into knots when I needed it most.

Or did I? Did I really need words right this moment?

Daddy got up and kissed me on the head. "Nope," he repeated, "I wouldn't blame them one bit."

I opened the magazine and lay on my bed, staring at that Canada goose family for the longest time. Suddenly I pictured myself and Crystal and Roxann as squawking goslings and Mama with her wings all spread out and flapping. And I couldn't help it. I laughed out loud.

Then I felt a wave of something. I think it was hope.

After all, Daddy hadn't just talked about squawking goslings with ruffled feathers. He had said, "These geese keep the same partners all through their lives."

FIFTEEN

It seemed like summer had just taken hold when the school bells started ringing again. I had a different teacher and different friends in a different classroom, but the routine was the same, and there was a comfort about that. Plus being away all day long made me feel a little happier about being home at night. And homework time meant writing time on a regular schedule. My journal was bursting with fresh ideas.

Daddy and Mama went on welfare, had no choice while they were searching for jobs.

Crystal was acting older now, talking older, too. "Ain't you getting sick of the lean times, Janelle?" she asked one Saturday morning.

"Sure," I answered. "I wonder what it'll be tonight." Every day we woke up with supper on our minds.

"Maybe spaghetti again," said Crystal, making lip smacks.

"If we get lucky," I hoped. My rumbling stomach got me out of bed.

"Umm, I can almost taste those meatballs rolling over my tongue," Crystal dreamed aloud.

Roxann groaned. "You two always make me hungry with your food talking. I'm telling!" She hiked up her nightie and ran to find Mama.

Truth is, the way things were lately, we learned to look upon a plate of pasta like gourmet diners look upon a shrimp cocktail, except we didn't eat with such slow and fancy manners, especially at the end of the month, when the money was gone. We knew by some kind of instinct that we'd better get our meal swallowed before it disappeared from right out under our noses.

It was the end of the month. It was easy to tell because all week long, our whole family kept bumping into each other, getting on each other's nerves looking into the cupboards all the time.

"Scoot," Mama kept saying. "Get your heads outa those shelves. Ain't gonna find a thing anyway."

"But I'm hungry," Roxann kept insisting. I figured she must be in a growth spurt. Glad I wasn't. I hoped mine would hold off until Mama or Daddy's name was on a payroll again.

Daddy said, "There's always a little something to fill you up at mealtimes."

"I don't want to wait till mealtimes. I want something *now!*" Roxann said.

"Me too," echoed Crystal.

Me too, I thought silently, knowing better than to speak it out loud.

"You all just got a touch of the Empty Pantry Syndrome," Mama said in a high-and-mighty tone.

She and Daddy started laughing and laughing until they doubled over.

"What's so funny about being hungry?" I asked when they were straightened back up again.

"Ain't nothing funny, Janelle. That's why we gotta keep laughing," Daddy said.

This particular riddle was way beyond me. This one needed some mulling-over time.

That morning we ate oatmeal, watered down. It wasn't great, but it was something. Lunch was tuna on one bread slice for everyone.

"Where's my sandwich top?" Roxann asked.

"There is no top," Mama answered. "It's called an open-face sandwich. Just eat it."

Daddy said, "Open face is right. Better open

your face and shove it in before somebody
else does."

I laughed at that, but I was chewing and it
made my jaw hurt like crazy.

SIXTEEN

Right before suppertime that same day, I got to worrying bad. I had just figured up the contents of the fridge. There was one shiny eggplant, a carton of milk, a touch of tomato sauce, and a bit of ground-up meat.

"Mama, what are we having for supper?" I asked. "There's only an eggplant—"

"Yuck! Eggplant!" Roxann shouted.

"You let me do the worrying about supper," Mama said, the kind of thing she always said whenever I got to worrying. Unpaid doctor bills were one thing. They didn't make my stomach clench and my mind get irritable.

"It's bleak," I said, and Mama had no response.

I sat down in the kitchen, trying to figure out why Mama would even say to me, "You let me do the worrying about supper." Because worrying, no matter who was doing it, wasn't going to fill five bellies.

I watched close, waiting for her to start preparing something from nothing. Mama caught on, because she called to all of us, "Girls, go on outside and find something to do."

"What's outside?" I asked.

"Go on," Mama ordered. She was wearing her don't-mess-with-me look. So I changed my mind and got my sisters and out we went.

I told Crystal about the food situation. "You're talking bleak," she said, "with a capital *B*."

"For sure," I said. "Mama will be needing the Mealtime Magician tonight!"

Babs and Linda and Veronica were drawing a chalk walk. So we added our own creations to the concrete for a while.

Suddenly a black-shoed, blue-trousered leg stepped over the rainbow I was drawing. Mr. Jefferson, the mailman. He said, "Nice work, girls," and handed me our stack.

"Thanks, Mr. Jefferson," I said. I dropped the chalk when I saw one of my envelopes.

I sat on the steps till I worked up the courage. Then I slid it slowly, carefully open. I unfolded the white sheet and read it twice before the words sunk in. A smile spread across my face.

Crystal dashed up next to me. "Is it good news? Is it another check? Are you getting another story published?"

Roxann and my friends all gathered round.

"They're holding it," I said.

"What does that mean?" asked Roxann.

"Stop talking riddles," Crystal said.

"It means they like it. It means 'maybe.' It's a start," I explained.

"A 'maybe' is better than a 'no,' " Babs said.

"You got that right," I agreed.

After the excitement wore down and we finished our chalk walk, my stomach started sassing me fierce.

Crystal went upstairs to go pee and came back out. "I smelled something cooking," she said.

"Where?" I asked.

She answered, "Right in our own kitchen."

"You must be having a nose mirage," I told her.

Just as I said that, Mama was rounding us all up for supper.

We washed our hands in a hurry and sat down and joined them together so Daddy could say the grace as usual. I watched him and Mama back and forth. They were trying their best to act normal, but I could tell something was up.

There was a steaming pan of saucy food in the middle of the table.

"What's this?" asked Roxann.

I craned my neck and recognized the seeds and the deep purple skin. I opened my mouth to tell Roxann, but before I could even say "eggplant," Mama gave me her warning look, and I shut it fast.

"It's Bagetti," Daddy said.

"What's Bagetti?" Roxann whined. "I never heard of that."

"It's like spaghetti, only a little different. Now eat," Mama said, smiling over at Daddy.

Crystal saw them and looked over at me.

They served us first, and did we gobble! Then they forked what was left right out of the pan.

Daddy sat way back in his chair and tucked his thumbs in his waist. "That Bagetti sure hit the spot."

"Best I ever tasted," Mama said.

Suddenly their cheeks exploded. They were hooting and howling like some crazy hyenas, doing that doubled-over laughing again.

Roxann giggled, but Crystal and me, we just stared.

That night in our room, Crystal and I whispered because of Roxann.

"She sure is sleeping sound," I said.

"Probably because she isn't hungry," Crystal said.

"Yep, must be that Mealtime Magician," I said.

We muffled our laughing in our pillows, and Roxann stirred, so we stopped altogether. We lay back on our covers, and before I knew, Crystal's sound-asleep breathing was coming slow and steady too.

Just as dozing was taking me over, whispering made me come awake. I listened close. My ears picked up the worry in Mama's tone.

"What about tomorrow?" she said to Daddy.

"We'll figure something out, I promise," Daddy said. "We always do."

"At least we have so far," Mama said.

There was a pause. Then Mama said, "Bagetti."

She and Daddy started laughing and laughing, just like they got to doing before. They tried muffling the sound, but they couldn't muffle the feeling.

The laughing was so catchy that I got it too. I squashed the pillow right onto my face and hushed as much as I could so I wouldn't wake up Crystal and Roxann.

Mama and Daddy's sides must be sorer than sore, I thought, holding my own.

Then I thought about Comfortable, and how it comes in different ways.

I thought about all kinds of hunger, and I knew the truth. Saw it flicker bright like a gleaming candle flame.

Crystal and Roxann were sleeping sound, but I had to share it, so I whispered to them soft, "Ain't no one ever gonna starve for nothing in our house, even when there is no food."

SEVENTEEN

Little by little, I started feeling like things were falling into their proper places. Good thing too, because fall settled in and that circle of annoyances would have otherwise tightened and strangled us all.

We celebrated Thanksgiving again at Aunt Barbara's. She outdid herself. Daddy said, "For a woman who hates to cook, you sure can pull together some fancy feast."

Aunt Barbara was pleased. "Nothing but the best for the best," she said. What a difference a year makes! I thought.

Daddy said the prayer. When he got done, Roxann said, "Daddy, how come you gave thanks for all our wealth when we're so poor?"

Daddy answered, "Money isn't what makes a person wealthy, baby."

Roxann looked at me and said, "What's that supposed to mean?"

I said, "It's a life riddle. Grown-ups have lots of them to explain things."

Roxann shrugged and went back to her chestnut stuffing and cranberry sauce.

Crystal said, "Too bad the life riddles don't do a better explaining job. I don't get it either." But I sincerely half understood that particular one.

The Saturday after Thanksgiving, Mr. Jefferson rang our bell. "I've got a certified letter for your father," he said.

Daddy signed with a flourish and couldn't wait to get back inside. He closed his eyes and took a deep breath. I knew exactly what he was feeling. We all stood around and watched him open it.

Mama was reading over his shoulder. The letter dropped and he let out a whoop and next thing we knew, Mama's feet were swinging through the air.

When Daddy let Mama come in for her landing, he gathered us all in a huddle. "Daughters," he announced, "you are looking at the new assistant manager of Hernando's Hardware Store."

Suddenly we were swinging round and dancing too.

At lunchtime Daddy said, "Feels like pigeons are doing air acrobatics in my stomach."

"You'll do fine," Mama said as she spread mayonnaise on all our sandwiches.

"I'm mighty tense; I've never been an assistant manager before. Matter of fact, none of my jobs has ever been in selling," Daddy said, "and Monday isn't far enough away."

"Daddy," I remembered, "anyone who can sell Roxann on an open-face sandwich is already a great salesman."

He touched my chin in that certain way with his finger, and at that moment I was surer than sure where we all belonged. I had that same feeling, not quite so strong though, when I'm putting a puzzle together and I find the missing piece under the couch.

That night I started another story called "The Missing Piece." It ached inside me like a nagging tooth, needing attention sooner than soon. I couldn't ignore it. It kept me awake. I switched on the bedroom light and put a T-shirt over it to make it dimmer. Crystal stirred and Roxann turned over, still sound asleep. Whew!

I was almost finished when Mama saw the light and came in. "Janelle, it's nearly one in the morning. What are you doing awake?" she whispered.

"Couldn't sleep," I said.

"Restless, huh? Me too, that and excited. Come on." She motioned me out to the kitchen. I brought my story with me. The floor was cold and made my whole self shiver. My feet found the chair rungs in a hurry.

"There. Now we don't have to be so quiet," Mama said. "This calls for some hot cocoa."

"You remind me of Aunt Barbara, Mama," I said. "All special events call for chocolate."

"Gee, I wonder why that could be." She chuckled as she poured the milk and got out the mix.

"Aren't you glad about the seesaw?" I asked.

"The seesaw?" she repeated.

"Yeah, going up in the clouds again," I said.

"The seesaw, of course!" She smiled, glad that I remembered the way she described living. "Yes, very glad, Janelle. It feels more balanced now."

"Yeah, I like the steady up-down pattern better than those big swoops and bumps," I said.

"You can say that again!" Mama said. "We've sure had our share of the bumps."

"But you know what, Mama? It doesn't hurt so much when we all get bruised together." I thought of that Canada goose family, all huddled together in a raging, roaring storm.

She shook her head and said, " You are something, Janelle. Really something."

I didn't know what, but I knew it was good. The hot cocoa wasn't the only thing warming me through and through.

"Sleepy?" Mama asked when we slurped the last sips from our mugs.

"Not yet," I said. "I'm gonna finish this."

Mama picked up my story. "May I?" she asked.

I nodded.

"The Missing Piece," she said out loud, then bit her lip and clicked her tongue and shook her head and sighed. She had tears in her eyes when she finished what I'd done so far.

"Aunt Barbara was right about writing it down," I said.

Mama set the mugs in the sink and sat back down. "Sleepy?" I asked.

"Not yet," she replied.

She pulled a sheet of blank paper out of my stack and smoothed it out on the table in front of her place. I saw love in her eyes when she stared at me. Then I saw the eagerness when she smiled. "Got another pencil?" she said.